D1569047

Afflicted

By

Nicholas. J. McKee

Afflicted

~~~~

*To my Mother and her mother, my
"Mom mom."*

~~~~

Table of Contents:

Prologue 1

Chapter One: Matthew 4

Chapter Two: Jack.......................................21

Chapter Three: Matthew 29

Chapter Four: Matthew...............................45

Chapter Five: Melissa 53

Chapter Six: Matthew..................................60

Chapter Seven: Jack....................................75

Chapter Eight: Melissa................................81

Chapter Nine: Michael.................................88

Chapter Ten: Matthew.................................94

Prologue

My skin still burns from yesterday. Her cigarette marks look like constellations on my arm. It doesn't bother me anymore though. I've grown used to it. Honestly, I don't think I cry from the pain anymore. I cry to please her. I know it sounds horrible. Why should I care about pleasing her? The woman who tries to kill me if I don't get her a beer. But she's my mother. I can't help but try to please her. I don't like her. Not a bit. But I love her.

Elaine told me she was going to sneak me out today, so I've been looking out the window waiting for her car all day. We're going to go get ice cream and see a movie. Then she's getting me new school supplies.

It's hot out today but I have to wear long sleeves. If Elaine saw the marks on my arm she would try and kill our mom. I promised her that she stopped doing it, so Elaine would lay off a bit. As much as I loved her protecting me it only made my mom angrier. And she always takes her anger out on me. She used to take it out on Elaine, but as soon as she turned eighteen she left. I don't blame her. I want to leave sometimes too. Well most of the time, but then there are times I don't. I want to stay when my mom's sober and tells me how much she loves me or tells me how smart I am, or even when she buys me a huggie from the corner store. And it's not her fault she's like this either. If my dad never left her, she probably would be sober all the time. At least I like to think so. As much pain as she causes me I would feel too bad about leaving her.

I saw Elaine's car pull up out-front. Hopefully my mom doesn't find out she's here. She doesn't like it when I leave with Elaine. She thinks she's going to take me away from her. Not that she would care too much. But it'is Sunday so she's probably sleeping off whatever it was she did last night. And if she does wake up she's most likely going to be worrying about her new boyfriend who she brought home last night. I don't usually like any of her boyfriends. They're all the same really. They smoke. They drink. And they hit my mom. I just stopped paying them any mind.

Elaine wrapped her arms around me as soon as I got in the car.

"So, what do you want to do first?" she said it so happily. I swear she could cheer the saddest person in the world up just by saying hi.

"Ice cream!" I said. We always ordered the same thing, chocolate and vanilla swirl with rainbow sprinkles.

I could tell it was going to be a nice day. It was always nice to escape from my life every once in a while...

Chapter One: Matthew

I laid there shivering in the cold and dark. Two thoughts were racing through my mind. Where am I? Why was I here? Honestly, I thought I was dying. I could feel my entire body throbbing in pain.

Everything was blurry when I opened my eyes. I couldn't hear much only a vague ringing in my ears like distant church bells. I kept trying to remember why I was here but the only thing I could concentrate on was the freezing cold. Suddenly I was telling myself to get up. But where was I going to be getting up from? I realized that I have the hood of my sweater wrapped around my head and so I slowly took it off to look around me.

I was in an alleyway. A long vast alleyway. In the distance though I saw what looked like silhouettes of people. I picked myself up—again at a slow pace to make sure I didn't tremble. Soon after I found myself walking towards the figures in the distance. I sighed in relief knowing I wasn't the only one here. In all, there were five people here. Gathered around a small bonfire in a trash can. I limped over realizing I could hardly feel my left leg.

"Where am I?" I said waiting for any response that would tell me why I was here. There was a man in a bright yellow jacket. Looking at him, I would never believe his voice would be as soft as it was.

"Well you got pounded by that one tall guy and then passed out for a few hours." I could feel myself looking at him incredulously. "Pounded?" I thought still in disbelief. Along with not knowing where I was I have no idea what my name was, where I lived, or if I even have a home.

But again, I asked, "Do you know where I am?"

"Devon, Wisconsin." Said a petite woman in pink. She spoke softly and had a raspy voice. Her long dangling earrings danced as she spoke.

"Do you know exactly how long I've been here?"

The same man in the yellow coat spoke again.

"About two hours ago we were sitting here when you came running from this big man, screaming 'help'." Now pointing to the lady in the purple hat the man in yellow continued.

"Marcie tried to figure out what was happening, but the man threatened her, and she got scared. The guy must have been twice your size, anyways he just grabbed onto your back and started hitting you until you passed out and then he ran away."

Disbelief was now an understatement. I started to feel the freezing cold rush down my back, so I rushed to put my hands in my pocket. In my pocket I could feel three objects. When I pulled them out there was a note, a key, and a pocket knife. I studied the note, it read "427 Mansfield St. Apartment 6." I handed the note to the man in yellow and asked where I can find this place.

"Marcie goes by there all the time she can take you there on her way to the market"

I asked her if that would be okay, she replied "ABSOLUTELY" with great enthusiasm. After she said goodbye we began to walk towards the street at the end of the alley way.

We were now at the spot I had woken up from and I glanced down to find a black wallet. I picked it up and opened it. Inside was a twenty-dollar bill and three cards. I pulled out the first card and it was an ID. The light from the moon caused a reflection on the card and for the first time I saw what I looked like. I was the same person as the one on the ID. This card alone finally gave some of the information I was longing for. My name was Matthew Green. I was 17 years old, five feet and eleven inches tall, my eyes were blue, and I was a resident of Wisconsin. I looked up and the girl named Marcie was tapping on my shoulder.

"What's your name anyway?"

"Oh, it's um uh Matthew" I said like I didn't just find that out..

"Swing left on this corner" Marcie said quickly. It must have been very early in the morning because there was no one in sight and the sky was blue and had a small glimpse of orange light. I asked her how much longer we were going to be, because I was still in agonizing pain but all I got was "Soon."

She began to ask me questions, but I only vaguely heard them. I was too busy wondering what was going to be in the apartment—or who. I still could not remember anything.

When I came back to reality I started giving her legitimate answers, it seemed like the best thing to do to pass the time.

"So, where ya from?"

"Uh Wisconsin, I guess."

"Is there anything else you know? not very talkative are ya." She let out a little giggle.

"Not really"

"Well I'm Marcie, Marcie Mangle."

"What were you doing back in that alleyway?" it seemed polite to speak back.

"Well that's my home. The guy in yellow, Ben's his name, he raised me since I was young. After my momma died early on he started looking after me."

Suddenly after she said those words I could see myself. But I wasn't myself I was a younger me. There was someone else there too. It was like a vision. Or a hallucination. I was hiding under a table in a pink kitchen.

It was dark but the moonlight coming through the window next to the refrigerator revealed a woman. Smoke like that of a cigarette was filling my lungs and I was coughing uncontrollably. She was screaming but I couldn't make out what she was saying. The woman was tall and skinny. Almost skinny enough to see her bones. She had short brown hair and big cheek bones. Then the vision was over, and it was back to walking with Marcie. I shook it off and told myself it was because I was dehydrated.

The sun was up now, and Marcie stopped to look at me.

"Your face really got banged up. There's a store on the corner a few blocks up. I know the people that own it. We can get you cleaned up there before we continue."

We reached the store and it was small and had a bright neon sign that read "Al's Quickie Mart." When we walked in the smell of fish hit me right in the face. Two people walked up to us. One was a tall wide man with greyish hair and mustache. The other was a short little lady with a very pale face and long black hair. The man must've been two feet taller than the woman.

"Hey 'Marc' who's this?" They sounded friendly.

"It's my friend Matt." She looked at me and faintly smiled. "We were wondering if we could use your bathroom?"

"Of course, honey anything you need, and how's Ben?" her voice shifted to sound concerned when she asked.

"Oh, same old same old."

We began walking down a very small and tight aisle, where at the end was a small white door. Marcie opened it to reveal a yellow stained toilet, a pink sink, and an overflowing trash can. She took a paper towel from the dispenser next to the sink, ran it under cold water and started rubbing it on my face.

"Hold still it might sting a bit." Her voice was so reassuring that it calmed me almost instantly. For just a moment in what seemed like days I was finally calm and for just that one moment my mind wasn't racing.

From the corner of my eye I could see her digging deep in her purse, and then she pulled out a small box. I tried to read it, but I didn't want to move my head too much. She pulled out a band aid and placed it gently over my forehead.

"How's that?" She asked this as though she just accomplished something impossible.

"Fine I guess." I replied the same way I've been for the past however long it's been.

We left the store and finally began to walk towards my destination, whatever it was that I was walking to. Until now I hadn't realized how decayed the houses looked in this neighborhood. Looking at them made me only more depressed. In fact, I wasn't really depressed I was more confused. I had no idea what was going on or what was happening. In just a few moments I was going to enter an apartment that for all I knew could be someone else's home. Again, my mind was racing.

"We're almost there" Marcie said quickly. I felt a pit in my stomach growing. It's all okay, I'll remember everything when I go in there. After this thought popped into my head, I felt that I could be calm about the whole thing. So that's what I'm going to keep telling myself. I realized how quiet Marcie got. She hasn't really said a word since the bathroom at that store. I wanted to ask how old she was, but I thought it would be rude.

I was trying to stay calm but couldn't bare the silence anymore. I was already a little nervous and I wanted to take my mind off of it. The impulsivity of my words took over me and I couldn't stop myself from talking. I was trying to fill the silence with anything I could, but now I was talking in spite of myself. I gasped for breath and then stopped. When I looked over she had a startled look on her face. But it quickly shifted to a comforting smile. She sat me down on a row of steps in front of us and laid her hand on my shoulder.

"When I was about seven years old, my mama died". She must have known what I was going to ask next because before I could get my words out she continued. "It was a drug overdose, she never really recovered after my dad walked out when I was two." Marcie stopped talking for a minute and looked down at her feet. Her eyes were wide, but I saw no tears. You can tell she's a very strong person.

"That's when Ben started looking after me. It's not an ideal situation but he's the best and only family I have." Now I was the one looking at my feet. I have no idea if I have any family and the thought of being alone in the world didn't scare me but made me feel depressed more than ever. I could feel my eyes start to water. Like when the freezing cold slaps you in the face. Though it wasn't the cold doing this, it was feelings. I was literally sad about being sad. Not that that makes much sense.

The next thing I knew I was leaping up off the step and wiping away the tears from eyes.

"Let's go." Without a reply Marcie jumped up and started walking.

We've been out for a while now because I noticed people walking around, and the sky was a bright blue.

We walked past a bar. Outside was a guy smoking a cigarette. He was short with dark black greasy hair. His thick beard and mustache almost covered his whole face. He stared at me for a couple of seconds and then with a low pitch voice said:

"You the guy Markie was beaten on last night. Yea, he said you was buggin on em and stole his phone." I glared incredulously at him for a moment until he spoke again.

"You oughta get out of here before he gets back." Marcie told me not to worry because she can take any man, and I believed her. She seems like that type of girl who can fight herself out of any situation.

We began to walk away, and I could still feel the little man's eyes on me. I had no idea what he was talking about though.

A new feeling distracted me from this. My throat started to feel dry and my stomach started to growl.

"When's the last time you ate?" Marcie asked. As if she was reading my mind.

"I'm not sure." I replied softly. My face was pale with fatigue. My stomach was burning with hunger and my body was numb.

"There's an IHop on Market Street a few blocks down. I'll pay, Marcie said." I just nodded and wondered with what money was she paying. She was literally living on the street. But I just followed her and said nothing.

It was ironic to me that I have no clue about any aspect of my life except my name and age, but I remembered what IHop was. It was funny, but ultimately made me sad again. I needed something to take my mind off what I was currently thinking and so I thought about Marcie's clothes. There were definitely going to be people staring at her in the restaurant. As if people weren't already. She wore a bright pink and purple shirt. She had a vibrant personality which went along with her clothes.

We were now close to the IHop because in the distance I saw a vast blue roof with an enormous "H" on the top. When we arrived the parking lot was less packed than I had expected. This was relieving to me because it meant less eyes were going to be on me. Well really on Marcie.

Marcie and I passed through a narrow doorway and followed a blue carpet to a tall lady at the front desk. Marcie did all the talking and I just looked around. There weren't many people here. It confused me because the inside of the building was much larger than how it looked on the outside. There were maybe ten tables in the entire restaurant not counting the five booths lined next to the windows. I glanced over to the pancake themed clock on the door that read *11:42 a.m.*

"Your table is ready." I followed the waitress and Marcie. She sat us in a booth next to the door.

"Can we start you with any drinks today?" The waitress asked politely

"Get whatever you'd like honey." Marcie said.

"I'll have a water... uh, please, Thank you."

"And you?" directing towards Marcie.

"A coffee with two sugars, and some cream please." I feel like Marcie may be the last person on earth who needs coffee.

"No problem."

Now it was just me and Marcie alone again. But I didn't feel awkward. She knew what I was feeling. Marcie broke the silence and started talking.

"Do you know the guy who hit you in the alley yesterday."

"No, Honestly I don't remember anything." She looked just as confused as I have been.

"I had just assumed you didn't want to talk." She said.

"The only thing I know is my age and name, and that's because they were on the ID in my wallet I found"

"How old are ya then?"

"Seventeen." I replied.

"You're just a child to be on the streets alone." This realization hadn't hit me until now. If I was this young I had to have parents somewhere. *Hopefully.* My life seemed a little less bleak now. I had more hope than before.

"Well hopefully you'll find some answers when you go to that address you found." She smirked and then continued. "Do you know what you want to eat? You can have whatever you'd like." I smiled just enough that my lips made a half circle shape and said the first thing that came to mind "Pancakes." Marcie giggled gently.

"I think I'll have the same thing, Marcie said." The waitress returned with the same bubbly and happy-go-lucky face she had before.

"Are you ready to order?" She towered over us casting a shadow over the table. Marcie replied with a soft and polite "Yes." We gave her our order, then the waitress again gave an enormous smile and made a fast turn. Her ponytail quickly followed behind. Marcie was fiddling with something in her pocket and so I glared out of the huge window next to me. It was a wide-open parking lot with not many cars. There also appeared to be a bus station on the sidewalk. I soon realized that I was heavily focusing on the cars going by. I could tell you the color of every car that went by for several minutes. It was peaceful. I glared back at Marcie now playing with a pocket watch. She knew I was watching her because she sighed and said, "It was my dad's." Looking despairingly, which was new for me to see because since we met, she hadn't shown a sad side. I thought she only had one emotion. Happiness. She continued, "He left this with my mom before he walked out. After she died it was the first thing I took. I know it's sad, why should I care but when I hold it I feel like I know him."

"I understand." I said. I don't know how I understand but I do.

Our food finally arrived and the look in Marcie's eyes was ravenous. I began eating right away and finished my pancakes within a few minutes. Marcie finished right after me and asked for the check quickly. She was just as anxious as me, or anxious for me. We picked ourselves up and exited after Marcie left the money on the table. We were both full after the meal we just had. Before eating I felt like I hadn't eaten in days.

The air was getting cooler outside, but it was still warm. "Just a few blocks down." I nodded and kept walking. I was intent on getting to that destination.

I realized while looking at Marcie that she walked so unusual. It was a sort of a skip and speed walk put together. It certainly fit her personality.

My head felt like it was vibrating, and it was racing. I could sense my breathing was getting heavy too. I stopped where I was walking and tried to regulate my breathing. Marcie didn't realize what I was doing because she was putting a flower she found on the last street behind her ear. I was finally okay and went to catch up with her.

"Oh, Thanks for breakfast today." I said happily. Marcie just looked at me and smiled.

"I remember being just as young as you are now. You'd think living on the streets so young would be a bad thing, but I couldn't have asked for a better life. I was, and still am free to do whatever I want." I kept smiling and stared at the ground as we walked. I didn't know what my life was like now, but a life of freedom sounded like just what I wanted. Looking at her vibrant personality, and the way she carried herself through the day, like nothing was ever wrong, gave me so much confidence that I could live like that too. I told myself that no matter what I found in that apartment I would try and live as free as possible for the rest of my life. Maybe it was just a pipe dream.

"We're getting really close now." Marcie said.

"Do you have any idea what you might find?" She asked intently. "No." I replied. In all honesty I haven't really given it much thought until now. It was sort of something I just had sitting in the back of my brain. We walked towards the end of the block and I could see a street sign that said *Mansfield.*

"This is it 427 Mansfield St." I sat out front staring at the gloomy grey building. I looked back to say thanks to Marcie, but she wasn't there. Normally this would freak me out, but I needed to know what was in that apartment. Walking up the steps gave me a worse feeling then waking up in the alleyway. I reached the door at "Apartment 6." There went the splitting headache again, not minding it I put the key in the gold door knob and opened it...

Chapter Two: Jack

I was in the doorway of an apartment. Why can't I remember anything? I'm just going to stand here for a while. I have no recollection of what happened before now. I'm alone. But I quickly remembered this happens often. It still didn't make me feel any better. The last thing I do remember was sitting in a doctor's office. The white lights in the office made everything seem blurry when I tried to picture it. There was a sign though, that read Dr. Mary Walker. It's the only thing I could make out.

Something in my head—More like a voice—was telling me to go into the apartment. I was hesitant but had no other options. So, I did.

I must've been here before because I was holding the key in my hand. I walked into the apartment. All the walls were painted grey. There is a couch, a cluttered desk, and a lamp in the first room. I walked over to the desk, and there lied a huge folder with the name Matthew Green etched on to it. The name sounded familiar, but I made no connections. When I picked the folder up slowly I could see the goosebumps on my arms. I felt them too. There was also the same name at the bottom of the folder that I saw in the doctor's office, Dr. Mary Walker. Under her name was an address. I wrote the address on a piece of paper and shoved it into my pocket.

I now found myself walking into the next room. A pit in my stomach was growing like a snowball rolling down a hill. It was just an ordinary bathroom. I looked at myself in the mirror and remembered my name was Jack. Jack, I kept saying to myself. But I still couldn't remember anything else. I continued to walk. My hands started to shake, and my feet were trembling. I knew something was wrong. There was feeling of fear and trepidation attacking me. The bedroom was still with no warning signs. I continued to move back. The kitchen was the last room. I slowly walked to the kitchen. I could see the black and white tiles from the hallway. I looked down at my feet and at the tips of my toes was a thick substance. The room was dark, so I didn't see what color it was. I looked up.

THERES A BODY! It laid there mangled and I shivered in fear. The body was of a girl. She has dark brown hair just like mine, except hers has a sort of silky appearance to it. The thing that scared me the most was she looked familiar.

I found myself standing in the blood that had seeped out of this girl's body. She had to be dead for a while because she was blue, and her eyes were milky. My fear crippled me, and I couldn't move. I heard a creek in the floor and jumped but it was just a cat. It must've got in through the open window. The cat looked just as terrified as me. I was scared of everything now. I was scared before finding this body but now my fear grew to something I could not control. I ran out of the apartment. Leaving the building seemed like the best thing to do. My next step was to find this doctor. I needed answers, or at least a safe place to go. I asked the next person I saw where I could find "77 Wickford Ave."

A short lady with stubby arms and legs told me to go down six blocks, make a left, wait for bus 56, and take it to Elmer St. then the office is on the next block. She looked at me like I was crazy. It was probably because I was so jumpy.

At this point I thought my fear couldn't grow any more. I was wrong.

I ran so fast down the next six blocks my eyes started to water from the wind hitting them. I stopped when I saw a police car across the street. My teeth rattled. I had just seen a dead body and said nothing. *I was like a criminal.* Whenever I think my stomach can't turn anymore. It does. My body was shivering. Not because I was cold but because I was uncontrollably scared. Everything, even my own shadow scared me to death.

I began to walk slowly down the next street to the bus station. I made a left on the street where the lady told me to and waited for the bus. There was an old wooden bench on the corner. Considering it looked like it was going to collapse I just stood there. I crossed my arms because it made me for a minute, feel safe, like someone was holding me. The sun started to go down and my fear returned. The thought of standing here alone, in the dark was horrible. Another thought was in my head now. If it was dark the doctor I was looking for could have went home. This was worse than standing here. Every possible bad scenario was painting itself in my head. Taunting me.

I reached in my pocket to hold the note with the address as a sort of reassurance— but wait there's something else. The object was a pocket knife. Quickly I pulled it out and flicked open the blade. It was stained with blood. It made me feel empowered and a little bit safe, but it toyed with my anxiety. I just found a body in an apartment that I had a key too, and now a blood-stained knife in my pocket. If I was the one who killed that girl, it would make a lot of sense. But I would never do something like that. Would I?

The bus finally pulled up and I realized I had no money. I looked at the bus driver and gave a forgiving look.

"Are you getting on?" the bus driver asked.

"I-I don't h-have any m-money." I didn't know what to do so I just stood there very still. He must have felt bad for me because he glared at me for a minute and then told me I could ride for free. I sighed in relief.

"T-thank y-you." I said just under my breath as I walked up onto the bus. There were eight people aboard.

I walked down to the back of the bus which was empty. Looking at a window I saw my reflection and realized I looked like a homeless person. I didn't realize it earlier in the mirror in the apartment. My shirt had rips in it and my hair was greasy looking and gross. This must be why I could feel everyone's eyes on me. I boarded the bus less than two minutes ago and I was already longing to be off.

I took my seat and carefully examined all of the other passengers. The man closest to me was very pale and had long hair. His bony arms hung over the back of the seat.

The bus came to a screeching halt and I jumped from my seat in terror. Two people began to walk off of the bus. I decided I should not stare anymore and so I watched what was happening outside of the bus.

"Next stop Elmer Station." The bus driver shouted. This too startled me as does everything. I waited in my seat watching the houses go by outside the window. It was peaceful.

Again, the bus came to a sudden stop. This time though I was a little less startled. I was ready, and I was aware. But it still didn't stop my anxiety and the pit in my stomach was still there.

I quickly walked off the bus and ignored the "Have a nice night," from the bus driver. I walked down to the next street watching out for figures around me, clenching the knife with a tight grip.

I saw the office. A mailbox at the end of the steps going up to the building read the numbers 77. The building was dark which meant the people must have left. I had nowhere to go and it was night. I asked myself if I should go back to the apartment, but for obvious reasons decided not to. I decided to go to the side of the building and sleep behind the trash cans until morning. The ground was cold, but I had limited options. I was so scared I may have peed myself, but everything to me was uncertain right now. Gripping the knife tightly I told myself I was going to be okay. Though how could any of this be okay? I laid down, put my hood up and crawled in a fetal position.

The ground made me shiver. I could hear figures—shadows—lurking in the distance. People or things moving in the night. Every voice in my head told me they were all coming for me. Now it wasn't the cold making me shiver. I needed to sleep though. I'll be safe while I sleep. That's the newest lie I was trying to convince myself with. I closed my eyes. One breath. Two breathes out. Three breathes and I felt my body release all it's tension. Suddenly I was falling fast asleep....

Chapter Three: Matthew

"Matthew, Matthew? Is that you?" a soft voice was speaking to me in my sleep. I abruptly woke up when I felt a hand on my shoulder. It was a familiar face, but I couldn't make it out. It was a woman. She had a full head of white short hair and was dressed in all black. I still couldn't remember anything. She knew my name though and I must have been here for a reason, so I asked if she could help me.

"Why don't you come in dear," she said.

"Umm Ok..." I replied. She might actually be able to help me. I followed her up the stone steps to a big brown door. It opened to show an office. In the front there was a desk and chairs lined up on the walls. There was also a door in the back behind the desk.

"Follow me." she led me to one of the hidden doors in the back. Pointing to a couch in the room she said "sit" very calmly.

"So, tell me what's going on?" She said this again in a calm and composed tone. It made me feel relaxed.

"I'm not really sure. I keep waking up in different places and I can't remember anything." I felt like I could talk to her. Like it was safe.

"Do you know who I am Matthew?" She said keeping her tone.

"No" I replied. She looks familiar, I just can't make any connections.

"I'm your doctor. Dr. Walker. I treat others like yourself, who suffer from a disease called 'Multiple Personality Disorder'. I try to help you control it." She stopped talking and pursed her lips for a second. Then continued.

"Do you know where your sister is? She's your guardian and is supposed to monitor your medicine." Sister? I was shocked.

"Yes, Elaine." She said.

"I don't know about that, but I remember opening a door to an apartment." This immediately struck my memory. Marcie! Where's Marcie I thought. Dr. Walker shifted her position to place her arm on my leg. She continued.

"I have an idea, I'll try a form of therapy to help you get over this... amnesia."

She asked me to lay down and relax my body. From the corner of my eye I could see her getting up. She walked over to a cabinet on the other side of the room. She opened it and took something out, but I couldn't see what it was. She walked back and moved her chair closer. From her pocket she pulled out a small cassette player, loaded it with a tape and hit the play button.

"Close your eyes. You are doing great. Picture a tree. The leaves are blowing away slowly. You're falling asleep. You can feel the tension leaving your body. The leaves are still blowing, and you feel a gust of wind go by you." I began to fall asleep. I was still somewhat conscious. In what sounded like miles away I heard Dr. Walker's voice. I don't know what she was saying but it was triggering my mind somehow because visions were flooding into my brain. Elaine, Melissa,

Jack, Michael, and EJ. These were all names racing around in my head.

I remembered my sister, Elaine. I suddenly wanted her so bad right now. Everything came flooding back to me so fast. I had three uncontrollable personalities. Jack was the newest one who was afraid of everything. Michael was the worst one. His anger could make him kill someone. His soul purpose was just to hurt people. The last was Melissa, she was least like me. She was smarter, and she always wanted to be in control. Melissa was mean, but she was created to be a sort of maternal figure for me. My birth mother was a drug addict and she's the reason I have the disease. She was the woman in my vision from earlier. My mind developed these personalities as a way of blocking the memories of my mother. Melissa was made to get me out of bad positions and to take control when I couldn't. Michael came into existence in order to fight for me. He's not afraid of anything. At least that's what Dr. Walker thinks.

My personalities control everything in my life. This isn't the first time something like this happened. They're the reason I have to carry a note with my address on it everywhere, or how I can't even go out on my own most of the time. Everything was so much clearer now. I want to go back to not knowing. Almost as much as I wanted to know before.

There were thousands of memories flooding into my head right now but the only thing I cared about was seeing Elaine. She was my big sister. She was always there for me. She was the person who saved me from my mother's abuse. My disease didn't stop her from taking care of me either. Elaine was everything I wasn't. She was caring, selfless. She was beautiful and had long brown silky hair. Her eyes were a piercing blue, like diamonds.

I still did not remember what caused me to wake up in that alleyway yesterday. I know some guy beat me up because I tried to steal his phone. When I thought about it, it gave me a pit in my stomach. Something had to be wrong.

I woke up from the daze that I was in and took a large gasp for breath. Dr. Walker rushed to me and asked if I was ok. I said I was fine because I truly was. I remembered everything. Well, almost everything. Besides my stomach telling me something was wrong I had no reason to believe it. I started walking to the door and Dr. Walker grabbed my arm to stop me. I told her that I needed to go find Elaine.

With her grip on my arm tightening, she said, "remember the trick we worked on with Elaine." Use it when you need to. It's often used for people with anxieties, but it helps with my disorder. I remembered how doing this made me feel safe. Elaine used to do it with me when I would get nervous or scared. It is when I concentrate on things around me. That's when I figured something out. I realized why Jack was created. And why he's so scared all of the time. He's scared so I don't have to be. I created him so that I wouldn't have to be afraid anymore.

I ran out of the building and towards my apartment. I knew I could find Elaine there. I sat on the corner waiting for a taxi. I wasn't far it was just that my leg was in pain again and I was in no shape to walk four miles.

Finally, a taxi pulled around the corner and I jumped in the street and flagged it over. I opened the back door and hopped in.

"427 Mansfield St, please."

"Yes sir." said the taxi driver.

I started to develop a massive headache. My eyes were becoming droopy. But this has happened before. One of my personalities was trying to come out. They force themselves out when they haven't been in control for a while. Flowers, cars, trees, and houses. I kept concentrating on the things around me. After a couple of moments my headache was gone just as the taxi was pulling up to the front of my apartment building. A smile ran across my face. It felt like a lifetime since I saw my sister. I wondered if her boyfriend would be there. EJ was like a gentle giant. He could be furious one minute and soft and compassionate the next. He just doesn't show it. Elaine is the only one who can really handle him.

I was very anxious. I figured it was because my sister was probably worried about me and I have to tell her what happened to me. I don't know much about why I was there. Or why I had a pocket knife and a note with my address on it in my pocket. I was wistful that these questions would all be answered when I saw Elaine. I was undoubtedly feeling many emotions and some with no explanation.

"Here we go, *427*." the cab driver said abruptly.

"Thanks." I quickly took out the twenty from my wallet and threw it into his hand. For a second, I could see him look at me hastily, but he immediately pulled off. I ran up the steps and the door was cracked slightly open. The apartment was still, and I couldn't hear anyone. The sunlight from outside peered into the room through the white curtains. From across the room I could see a folder with my name written across it. There was a paper titled "DID" (dissociative identity disorder). The paper talked about medications and therapies. It didn't bother me because the only thing on my mind was seeing Elaine. I walked towards the kitchen in the back of the apartment. I thought Elaine might be sleeping. The apartment was so still and quiet.

I entered the kitchen, and immediately fell to my knees. Laying in a pool of blood was Elaine. I didn't scream because I was gasping for air. It was like my throat was being squeezed and my lungs were being crushed. It stopped for a few moments because it felt unreal. *It isn't real.* My hands were shaking faster than I could think. This wasn't real. THIS WASN'T REAL. I wished so much for this to not be real. I needed her here. I NEED THIS TO NOT BE REAL.

I rushed over to hold her. She was cold. Like ice. I cradled her in my arms while sobbing hysterically. "Everything is going to be okay." I kept telling myself this. I know I was wrong, but it was the only thing stopping me from doing something crazy. I looked down at my hands and clothes and I was covered in blood. I laid Elaine's body down gently and ran to her bedroom. Tears were flying down the sides of my cheeks. I grabbed her cell phone off of her night stand and a change of clothes and went into the bathroom. I stared at myself for a minute in the mirror and wiped the tears from my face. How and why did this happen? It was no use because no one knew the answer to that question. I changed my clothes as fast as I could and wiped my hands and arms with wipes so that I didn't stain anything else. I knew I would have to come back here and I didn't want to be reminded of this as much as possible. When I was done I dialed 911 on her phone and told them my address, and that I had found my sister in my kitchen *dead*. I was calm because I was now in a sort of shock. It seemed like there were steps to finding someone you love dead. First you lose your breathe. Second you sob. Third you're in complete shock. I was begging for there not to be a fourth step.

I figured I should pack a bag in case Elaine's boyfriend EJ takes me in since I was technically still a minor. WAIT EJ! He has no idea what happened. I snatched the phone out of the pocket in my sweater and dialed his number.

"Hey, I've been worried sick. You haven't called in two days."

"No EJ it's me Matt." My voice was cracking. Please come over quick it's my sister. Hurry I need someone." I hung up quickly, so he wouldn't ask any questions and began to go pack my bag.

Whenever I walked by the kitchen I looked the other way because I couldn't bare seeing her there. I started throwing stuff into my bag. When I went over to the dresser in her bedroom I saw a picture of the both of us and added it to the bag. I didn't look at it for too long, I didn't want to start crying again. I needed to keep my composure.

The living room was my next stop. The folder with my name on it and all the other important documents on the desk, that my sister had were all shoved into my bag. The first person to arrive was EJ. He came in the door so fast he looked like a blur. We exchanged eye contact right away and without words he had some sort of inkling as to what was going on. I dropped to my knees and cried uncontrollably. As much as I wanted to conceal my tears I couldn't. The horrible truth was that I was broken now. In just a short period of time my entire world fell apart.

"Where?" EJ asked just loud enough to hear. He knew. He had to know.

"The kitchen." I said

He left the room for a minute and when he came back he embraced me and I could hear a small whimper from him. He was broken too. But not like me. I had no parents. No aunts, uncles, or grandparents. I was alone now. On my own.

The police and the ambulance finally arrived. I was still on the floor wrapped in EJ's arms. The police asked us to step outside and wait for them to take the body out. I thought they had no sympathy for the situation. Just asking me to leave my home. EJ got up to go talk to the police but I stayed. I needed to see them take her out.

Four different EMT's came in, two were carrying a stretcher. I wasn't sobbing anymore but I could feel the tears running down my face. A few moments later, which felt like a lifetime, they rolled her out on a stretcher. I got up and ran to it. It seemed so inhumane just putting her whole body in a bag like that.

"NO... STOP. DON'T TAKE HER. PLEASE." I threw myself on the bag and wrapped my arms around her body. I know they have to, but I also know that when they do it will be all to real.

No amount of pain could equal what I felt in this moment. EJ came over and pulled me back. He was so selfless in this moment. He had just lost the closest person in his life too and was totally focused on me. But I don't care. I don't care about being selfless. Not when the one and only person I had, the only person I truly loved on this earth was gone now.

"We have to go." EJ said softly. I didn't reply. I simply got up grabbed my bag and walked out of the door. I know I would have to come back. I was coming to the realization that this place was only causing me more pain right now.

EJ locked the door when everyone left. He had an old black car with grey seats. I sat in the front seat and waited to leave. Everything was going so fast I just decided to follow all directions given to me. I wanted anything but to be here right now. His house was only up the street, so it wouldn't be a long ride.

Again, my head started to rattle, and my eyes became blurry. This usually happens when another alter wanted to take over. I just stayed calm and glared out the window. Tree, car, clouds. Tree, car, clouds. I noticed I was squinting really hard after a few seconds, so I relaxed my face and slouched into the seat.

The car ride was awkward, but it was quick. I could see the pain in his eyes too. He was also in shock. I threw myself out of the car when we arrived and walked up the path to his house. EJ unlocked the door and told me my room was the second one on the left, upstairs. He ran his hands through his hair and sighed. His life was falling apart just as mine was. I wondered how he was so calm and I realized it was because he didn't like showing his emotions in front of others. The only person he did that with was Elaine. But she was gone now. He was like me, afraid of accepting that she was gone. I didn't accept it. I just pushed it away. I had to think of what I was going to do next. For now, I decided to go up to my new room. It was a guest bedroom since EJ lived alone. It was small, but it was all I needed right now.

I decided I needed a bath. I don't have enough energy to take a shower.

I grabbed some clothes from my bag and took them with me to the bathroom. I slowly removed each article of clothing from my body and with them the blood and tears they had collected. I turned the water on and waited until the steam rose from the water and the mirror on the vanity fogged up. Lying my body down in the hot water made every muscle I had relax. I closed my eyes and descended my body to the bottom of the bathtub. My mind was dark for a moment.

Out of the darkness I started seeing things; Visions. There was Elaine. I wanted to hug her, but I couldn't. My hands started to shake, and I began crying out. Tears were once again streaming down my face. I regulated my breathing and then stopped sobbing. She wouldn't want me to cry.

I heard footsteps near the door and EJ entered. "What's wrong?" He was confused but I told him I was fine. I didn't want him to see me like this. Not in this amount of desperate pain. I didn't care that I was naked and totally exposed. I cared that I was broken, and I looked like it. He looked down on me. His face showed so much sorrow. I looked back at him and my eyes told him what my words couldn't. He turned around and shut the door. Until tomorrow morning I needed to be alone.

I lifted myself out of the bathtub and wrapped a towel around my body. After I dried myself off, I put my clothes on. They smelled like Elaine. Maybe it was just the laundry detergent that she used when she would wash my clothes, but I felt for a second like she was here with me. It was a warm feeling. Like just for a second the pain from her being gone was dissipating.

I turned the lamp off on the nightstand and laid down. I felt my body sink into the mattress. After I pulled the covers up to my neck all the tension ran away. A single tear swam down the side of my cheek, but I didn't start to cry. I was sad, but I was trying my best to be strong. For Elaine I guess.

I laid there staring at the white ceiling, just barely illuminated by the moonlight coming in through the window. Finally, I fell into a lonely black abyss and was asleep.

Chapter Four: Matthew

Sunlight drowned the room. It was peaceful as I started to awaken. I was in perfect harmony. *For just a minute.* Then it all came rushing back. Everything. Waking up in the alley. Elaine being dead. All the blood. I laid paralyzed in bed. If this was what every morning was going to be like I wouldn't be able to handle it. It was the most bittersweet few moments I've ever experienced. I closed my eyes quickly and took a deep breathe. The alarm clock on the nightstand told me it was 9:30 a.m.

In the distance just outside the door I heard a creek in the floor. Then heavy footsteps. The door knob opened and EJ came in and shot a sharp look at me. Not a scolding look though. "Get up we have to go." He spoke tersely, but nonetheless I had a feeling of where we were going.

I had just found my sister dead in my kitchen and police were definitely going to ask questions.

Who did it? I found myself asking the most basic question I could. Then I was thinking why I didn't ask myself this earlier. To be totally honest I don't really want to know. Whoever it was that did this I'll never forgive, or even be able to look at. Who could kill someone like Elaine? Someone so gentle and loving like Elaine. What could she have possibly done?

When my mind stopped racing I decided it was time to get ready and face the day. I put my clothes on quickly and walked down the steps to the living room. There I found EJ sitting on a chair in the corner with his face in his hands. I could hear the soft whimpers leaving him from across the room. I walked over, and he wiped the tears from his face quickly. It was no use, I placed my hand on his shoulder and told him it was ok.

EJ began to speak.

"Right before... You know." Oh, I knew. "She was gonna tell me something. She kept going on and on, the night before about something she had to tell me. She said it was going to change our lives. She told me it was 'Fantastic news.'" A faint smile ran across my face. Fantastic was Elaine's favorite word. She tried to use it in every sentence. He continued,

"I'll never know what that was now. I'll never hold her or be able to embrace her ever again." I glanced out the window because I couldn't look at him and not break down right there. I don't know why, but I had an inkling as to what it was she was going to tell him. I couldn't bear the thought of it being true though. If Elaine was pregnant then... then I don't know what I'd do.

"We have to go." He said abruptly. "And if they ask I will accept full guardianship of you... if that's what you want." I nodded and turned around.

It was a nice day outside. The sun was out, and it was warm.

We went outside and got into the car. There was a picture of Elaine on the dash. I don't know how I didn't notice it yesterday. I must've been to frantic to have noticed. She was smiling in the picture. Her smile was infectious and even through the picture it made me tingle from the inside out. She could turn the meanest person nice just by shooting a smile at them.

EJ started the car. He didn't look at the picture and I thought this was a good thing because if he had it just would have made the next few moments even harder than they already were.

It was now 11:13 a.m. and I was dreading talking to the police. It was so wrong what they were doing. The day after I find my sister dead and they have to do this. My biggest fear right now was crying in front of them.

I saw the "Twelfth district police station" sign and gulped. EJ pulled the car into a spot directly in front of the doors. Right as I was getting out of the car EJ grabbed my arm and said, "Everything is going to be ok." His voice was distressed. I looked directly into his eyes and then turned away. I walked towards the glass doors of the station and felt the warm sun hit the back of my neck. EJ's reflection shone on the glass as I opened the door. He was pouting. But then again who wouldn't be.

There weren't many people here. Just two police officers at the front desk. On either side were two tall steel doors. The barred square windows only made it seem so much gloomier. The lady at the front desk looked up at us and said "hello." Her voice was scratchy and low. EJ advanced in front of me. I'm not sure what he was saying, but he looked back at me and told me to come towards him. I moved slowly. The police officer closest to the door left of the front desk glided his hand towards the door. He led me into a small grey room. It consisted of only a table and two chairs. I slid into one of the chairs and clasped my hands over my lap. A woman I hadn't seen when we arrived walked in. She was a tall woman with short black hair. I've never seen a CIA agent before, but if I had to guess that's what they might look like. She laid a black briefcase on the table, sat down in the chair across from me, and smiled.

"Hi, I'm Miranda. I'm a social worker." Her words and body language were serene. Like she put no effort into moving or speaking, or anything.

She reached her hand across the table and asked what my name was.

"Matthew." I know she knew that already, but I wanted to comply with whatever she said.

"You're seventeen, now right?"

"Yes." I replied. She heard the despair in my voice and she shifted into a slouching position and sighed.

"I understand what you're going through. When I was seven I lost my mom to cancer." I wanted to tell her to skip the whole self-aggrandizing, I came-up-from-nothing and don't-throw-your-life-away speech, but I just stayed silent and let her speak.

"It was just me and her until she died. I went into the system for a few years and got adopted around ten. That's why I decided to become a social worker." I could feel a tear about to stream down my face in spite of myself. Even though I didn't want to listen to her it still hit close to home.

"I have EJ." I said gently. "He's going to take care of me." I said. I know he will.

"EJ was your sister's boyfriend?" She asked.

"Uh, Yea. He's twenty-five." She nodded and stood up. She walked over towards me and caressed my shoulder.

"If you need anything, and I mean anything call me." She handed me a card with the name "Miranda Shillings" and a phone number below it. I stuffed it into my pocket and stood up. From the side of my eye I could see her exit the door. When I turned around EJ was sleeping in a chair in the waiting room. His head was down, and his hands were folded on his lap. Then another person appeared in the doorway. It was a man. His head was bald, and he was dressed in a blue shirt and black pants. His badge reflected the ceiling light straight into my eyes. He was a police officer. He came over and shook my hand half-heartedly.

"Hi, I'm detective Charles, but you can call me Charlie." His voice was deep. He leaned on the side of the table and looked back at me.

"I understand you suffer from a mental disability? Multiple personalities is it?"

"Yes." I replied. I thought he was a bit insensitive, but I didn't mind. People usually don't know what to say or what to ask. He changed the topic.

"Were you close with your sister?"

"Very."

"You never fought, or tried to hurt each other, at all?"

"No." I said sharply. I knew what he was getting at. He thinks I did it, or at least he suspects me, but I didn't. I could never. I loved Elaine.

"Do you know anyone that would want to hurt Elaine?" He asked.

"No." No names came to mind.

"She was such a kind and gentle person. Who would want to hurt her?" I couldn't stop myself from getting a little defensive. I wanted to know who it was just as much as anyone else. I think. Honestly, I'm not one hundred percent sure on what I want.

"We'll be in touch." He said, and he walked through the big iron door. I looked back at EJ and then got a massive headache out of the blue.

Chapter Five: Melissa

Imbeciles! That's exactly what they are. I crossed my legs and laid my hands on my lap. What would possess Michael to stab her. Even worse than that Matthew has no idea. We have to get out of here and soon!

I saw EJ, Elaine's boyfriend, from the corner of my eye. I don't want him to find out it's me. I stood up and walked out. On my way through I made sure to shoot a nasty look at the police officers.

"Get up. we have to go." I said. His attire was that of a bum. I can't believe he would leave his home looking like that. And it's not like he can't afford nice clothes. His family is very wealthy.

"What's with your voice?" He said.

"Oh, um nothing." I changed my tone, so he doesn't suspect anything. He shook his head to wake himself up and then followed behind me. I despise the way he kept his dirty blonde hair so untidy.

We proceeded to get in his car. It reeked of sweat and mildew. On top of that the car was so hot I was choking. Thank God the seats aren't leather. I immediately calmed myself when he entered the car. He sat down and let out a sigh. I could smell his misery. He just kept going though. If I'm being honest I kind of admire that. His strength and will power, I mean.

Out of nowhere, and by the grace of God a plan came to me. When we get to EJ's I'll give control to Matthew, he'll obviously want to attend the funeral. After that I'll make Jack take over and force him to run away. It was perfect. A win-win situation.

We were finally back at EJ's. He stopped me before I could race out of the car. He grabbed my arm tightly. I must say it hurt a bit. Nonetheless he looked straight into my eyes, and just for a second, I saw beyond the unkept large man and saw what was really inside. Someone who was extremely broken. When he looked at me I could feel him looking into my soul. I didn't like it. I prefer it when people presume that I'm unsentimental. But for a moment I wasn't the cold and lonely person everyone else saw. For the first time in my existence I felt safe. Like I could let my guard down. The feeling was brief but felt like forever. Just then EJ started speaking again.

"While you were talking to the social worker and police officer I called around. Tomorrow we're going to have a ceremony at a funeral parlor and if it's ok with you." He gulped and then continued. "We'll have her cremated." I had no idea what to say. I didn't want to strip this huge choice from Matthew. I may be mean and cold but I'm not evil and I wouldn't do that to Matthew. He deserves to make that decision. I just said, "Can I sleep on it?" It sounded like something Matthew would say, so I went with it.

I wiggled my arm out of EJ's hold and exited the car. EJ went in front of me and opened the door. The home was a bit tidier than I had expected. EJ walked out of the foyer and into the first-floor bathroom. While he was doing that I ran into the kitchen and searched for a pen and a piece of paper. I scoured the entire room until I saw a slip of white hanging from a counter drawer. I ran over and opened it. I asked myself if my eyes were deceiving me. The drawer consisted of the biggest mess I've ever seen. Which in my mind is saying a lot because I share a body with a filthy teenage boy. There's no time for organization I told myself. I grabbed the paper and the pen above it. While I was in here I decided to look in the refrigerator for a bottle of water. Tap water is one of my biggest pet peeves. It just tastes gross. I grabbed a bottle of water. Now that I have everything I need, I began to power walk my way upstairs.

Then it hit me. What room is mine? I'll just check all of them and see if there's any signs of Matthew's belongings in any of them. There are four doors. Three on the left and one on the right. The one on the right was open and showed a bathroom. It was clean too from the looks of it which gave me a shot of joy. I tiptoed over to the first door. When I opened it, it was just a room filled with boxes. I had to leave immediately because the room was filled with dust. I slowly opened the next door which had a bed, a night stand, and a small armchair in the corner next to the window. When I looked down I saw a black backpack. It was Matthews, and on the bed laid his sweatpants. I was again pleased with how tidy the room was.

I went over to Matthew's bag and began to fold all the clothes in it. Underneath a white t-shirt I felt something hard. It was a picture. The picture was of Elaine and Matthew. I could feel my lip start to curl. I was always quite fond of her. More importantly she was Matthew's everything. Even though Matthew and I don't usually speak to each other I can sense what he's feeling most of the time. I set my sympathy to the side for a moment and kept doing what I had to. There are a few other things we're going to need, but we can get them on the way.

My plan is to take a train to Lakewood and hide out there. It's rural, and no one would think to look for us there.

Elaine had about ten thousand dollars put away which could get us pretty far. We just have to go to a bank on our way out of town. I zipped the bag up and moved over to the nightstand and placed the piece of paper down.

I wrote Matthew a little note to keep him up to speed. I kept it short and didn't tell him about the plan. I know that if he's aware about it he would do everything in his power to stop it. But it was the right thing to do. I needed to save Matthew. To keep him safe from all harm. If anyone found out that it was Michael who killed Elaine, Matthew would be done. They would take him away. Hurt him even. I couldn't allow it.

I realized how disgusting my clothes were and I would never lay in a bed in my own filth, so I changed. Matthew should be grateful his clothes will be color coordinated for once.

I prayed that EJ wouldn't come in tonight because I want to go straight to sleep, but you know, speak of the devil and he shall appear. I swear he was relentless. When I heard him coming I threw the blanket over the backpack and grabbed the note.

"Tomorrow morning, I need your answer, so I can meet with the funeral parlor." I nodded and then he turned back around. I heard a sigh and then he left the room. It was quite rude if you ask me. He didn't even knock when he came in.

I arranged the note next to the alarm so that Matthew would see it when he woke up. Then I stuffed the backpack under the bed and laid down. I liked staring at the ceiling before falling asleep. It was peaceful, and it helped me think better. I turned the light off and closed my eyes.

Chapter Six: Matthew

Waking up was the same as it was yesterday. I have a feeling it's going to be the same routine for a while. A few moments of bliss and then out of nowhere the excruciating pain of Elaine being gone. It's like a car hitting me from behind. Over and over again. I leaned over to see the time on the alarm and saw a note.

"Dear Matthew,
Your sister's viewing is tomorrow. She's going to be cremated, but only if that's okay with you. Whatever you should decide, make sure to tell EJ. He didn't know it was me in control yesterday, so I told him that I would make the decision today.

Very truly yours,
Melissa"

Just the name at the bottom made me cringe. Melissa was cold and mean. But this time she was different. She left me to make my own decisions. I respected that. I wasn't worried about her now though. Elaine's funeral was the only thing on my mind. I went down the stairs into the living room. Everything was still, and I got a pit in my stomach. It was just like when I found Elaine. I heard something in the dining room that shifted my attention. I let out a low sigh because it had to be EJ. When I walked in he was sitting at the table with a stack of papers. I didn't have to say anything because he saw me from the corner of his eye.

"Have you made your decision yet?" He asked.

"I'm really fine with whatever you do." I replied. I hadn't given it much thought but as long as I could see her one last time anything would be fine.

His pride was holding him back from tearing up. He just ran his hands through his hair like he usually does when he's thinking.

"I figured we could have a viewing and then cremate her." It sounded cold-blooded. Just talking about her like she was some object. I guess that's what happens when you die.

I realized I wasn't crying anymore. I was just *being*. I was existing in a world without the only person who ever really loved me, or that I loved.

I didn't want to think about it anymore. I shook myself out of the daze I was in and walked into the kitchen. I wasn't hungry, but I was thirsty. My throat was itchy and dry. I just grabbed a cup from off the counter and filled it up with tap water. I usually would do this when I would take my medicine. Elaine wasn't here to make me take them though and so I didn't bother. Besides I hated that medicine. It made me "loopy" and depressed. Not depressed like how I feel now. Depressed like if I don't get out of bed ever again no one will notice. Everything moves slower when I'm on it. And my brain gets fuzzy.

I really liked EJ's house. Our neighborhood was "Up and Coming" but EJ has one of the nicest houses in the neighborhood. EJ's family is wealthy and his father owns most of the homes around here.

Me and Elaine had only lived here for about two years. She worked hard to afford our apartment. We were never handed anything. Well, except extreme trauma and a horrible childhood. But that's what I always admired about her too. She had just the same life as me, instead she was stronger and attempted to do something with her life. Her *short* life. She worked hard to become what she was. She was an assistant at a law firm. And she sure had the brains for it.

"If you want there's some cereal in the pantry." EJ shouted from the other room. I still wasn't hungry though. He walked into the room slowly. More like he was dragging himself.

"Elaine's service is going to be tomorrow. It's the only time they had for the next few weeks." I just nodded and said ok. Who would be able to come on such short notice? Now that I'm thinking of it not many people come to mind that she was friends with. Her whole life was pretty much me, work and EJ.

"What time?" I didn't really care, I would be there no matter what time. I just wanted to break the silence.

"Uh, six o'clock."

"Oh, I was wondering." I stopped him as he was walking out.

"After the service would you go back to the apartment with me, so I could get a few things?" I noticed I was staring down at my feet.

"Yea whatever you need." He smiled. I felt a tingling sensation run down my back. It was a happy feeling. Like someone really did care about me. He turned away and walked into the next room.

I suddenly, out of the blue, craved a Pepsi. It was probably ten in the morning and I wanted a Pepsi so bad. I realized that I haven't been eating and drinking like I used too. Before everything happened, I had no less than a glass of Pepsi a day. Elaine would tell me to think about what it would do to my teeth if she were here. She always was a stickler for that stuff. I remember I found a pack of my mom's cigarettes when I was thirteen. I lit one up just to try it. Of course, my mom didn't care. In fact, if she had known she might have given me more. Anyway, Elaine walked in my room and started hitting me with a cooking magazine. My mother had never noticed I subscribed to a cooking magazine. Whenever I envisioned my future I always thought I'd be a chef. It's probably just a fantasy now. Not many places would take a high school dropout. I felt an unintentional smile on my face. What I would do for Elaine to be back. Just to hear her voice again. To have my life back on track.

When I was done in the kitchen I went back upstairs. I wanted to go to the store a few blocks down, so I was going to get changed.

I saw my new bedroom in a whole new light now. I never really noticed how nice it was. This is a big deal for me because I never had a nice room. Most of my life I shared a room. Or slept on the couch. I ran my hands on the walls and took in everything. There was a huge window on the one side of the room. You could see the city skyline out of it. It was beautiful.

The weather was nice out today. There was a cool breeze and the sun was out. I'd forgotten what odd weather we have here. It's sunny and warm out one day then freezing the next. EJ would always go on rants about global warming and stuff. He's a lot smarter than most people think. He's not just your average "jock." That's what Elaine always saw in him. She had a certain proclivity for seeing the best in people.

When I was ready to go I told EJ what I was doing. At first, he seemed startled. I guess he didn't think I was going to do anything but sulk all day. He got over it though and I left. There were a lot of people out today. I caught myself smiling at this one elderly couple on their porch. It made me enjoy life more. Seeing them made me see that not everyone's life ends the way Elaine's did.

When I walked in the store it smelled like cupcakes. I remembered they had a bakery in the back. Elaine used to get a pound cake every week from them.

On the wall on the other side of the counter was a huge refrigerator. I grabbed a cold Pepsi out of the fridge. It cooled my whole body when I touched it

When I walked to the counter the lady who owned the store looked at me dolefully. When I placed my hand on the counter she grabbed it and held it. Normally I would pull my hand back if a stranger just grabbed it like she did. I didn't though. She looked straight into my eyes. Which now that I think of it has been happening a lot lately. I guess people think that if they look you in the eyes the pain over your dead sister goes away. I don't know.

This was different though. It felt like she was healing me. Like just from touching me she gave me back a piece of myself. Maybe she's a witch or something. Elaine always believed in that stuff.

"How are you?" She had a rough crackled voice and an accent. Se continued.

"I know what's been going on, remember that there's always a silver lining." 'She was making me feel again. For the past few days I've been living sort of numbly. Just barely living. It would still be a while before I could live life normally again, but this was a start.

When I reached for my money she said "No." Still keeping eye contact with me she put the Pepsi into a small black plastic bag and handed it to me.

The air was clear. I was in a *happy mood*. Not *happy*. There's a difference. On the side of the pavement where I was walking was a patch of cement with an awning. It was a recreational building because the park was across the alley. I decided to sit down for a while.

The ground was cool where I was sitting. I leaned against the wall of the building. The stone slabs on the side were cool too. I shut my eyes and took a sip of my Pepsi. For just those few moments everything washed away, and I was content.

———————

I woke up to the sound of EJ's voice. He was shaking me vigorously. My guess was that I had fallen asleep for a while.

"It's four o'clock! What were you doing for 5 hours?"

"I needed some time to myself." I didn't know what to say, so I said the first thing that came to mind.

"Well whatever your reasons, we have to go. Your sister's service is in two hours." He seemed anxious. I bolted up after he said that. I had honestly forgotten. Elaine's viewing was the top thing on my mind now.

We went back to EJ's and I took a shower. The water was cold, but I didn't care. I was focused on seeing Elaine. I needed to hold her in my arms again. Just to see her. I know she won't be the same, but I don't care. I threw on a pair of jeans Elaine bought me. I didn't like them, but I never liked anything she bought me. I put them on to please her.

As if she was looking down on me. I know it sounded like a cliché, but I wanted to do little things, like wearing clothes she bought me, so I could feel close to her.

The clock on the nightstand read 5:14. I got dressed quickly and went downstairs. EJ was just sitting on the armchair staring at the grandfather clock in the corner.

"I'm ready." I said. I stood at the bottom of the steps and waited for him to get up. I could tell he was in a sort of *funk*. He picked himself up and followed me outside.

We didn't say a word to each other the whole way there. It wasn't awkward though. The silence I mean. We were just both thinking. Probably about the last time we saw her... alive.

When we walked into the funeral parlor EJ went to talk to the people who work there. I saw Elaine's casket at the front and ran to it. When I got about two feet away I stopped myself. A single tear ran down my face. I started to walk slowly towards her again. There she was. She was dead, but she was still beautiful. She looked like my mom. My mom was beautiful too. Even through all the years of drugs she was still beautiful. Elaine's silky long brown hair cascaded around her shoulders. I noticed they put makeup on her. She never needed to wear makeup. She was pretty enough without it. Fortunately for her she was secure enough to not want to wear it. Her hands laid crossed on her stomach. I placed my hands on hers. Her hands were cold and hard, and felt fake. Like a barbie doll. I still held them tightly though. Tears were streaming down my face. I saw EJ out of the corner of my eye. He was waiting to do exactly what I was doing now. Hold her. I wiped the tears from my eyes and kissed her on the forehead. I would be back to say my goodbyes later.

There was a chapel in the back and that's where I was going. There were pictures displayed all over of her. I just fell to my knees on one of the pews and continued to sob. I was gasping for air in spite of myself now. I didn't want to, but I couldn't stop.

EJ came in and told me people were starting to arrive. I got up and walked back towards her casket. I was trembling but kept moving. We stood in front of the casket side by side. About fifteen people shuffled into the room. This is the only funeral I remember being at, and I didn't know that everyone wears all black. A group of four women came up first. I didn't really pay attention to what people were saying. I just nodded and said thank you.

People kept coming in and coming up to the front to give their "condolences." I stayed quiet and let EJ do all the talking.

When I looked up Marcie was here. She was standing in the doorway in her vibrant pink tutu. I wiggled my way through the crowd of people near the casket and went towards her. She was holding a small grey box.

"How did you—?" She stopped me.

"I saw it in the paper, how are you?" She looked at me for a second and then gave me a hug. At first, I hardened up, but then I embraced her. I held her tightly and I didn't want to let go. I only knew her for a short period of time, but I felt close to her. She moved back and handed me the small box.

"Open it when you get home later." I nodded and walked back to EJ. Marcie left and all I could think about was seeing her again. EJ didn't see me talk to her because he asked me where I had went. I could see this whole thing was making him exhausted. He looked dogged. His eyes were droopy, and he was standing kind of slouched.

The people who own the parlor told us we only had about a half hour left. And so, I needed to say my final goodbye.

Going towards Elaine's body now was agonizing. It's the last time I'm ever going to see her. Every step was a little bit harder than the last. I finally got there, and tears were streaming down my face like a waterfall. It felt like all the air was being sucked out of the room and I was gasping. EJ was standing behind me with his hand on my shoulder. I couldn't help but scream "NO." It was almost involuntary. Now the weirdest thing started to happen. I was laughing uncontrollably. I sounded like a hyena. I couldn't stop though. EJ's face was puzzled. I had no idea why I was doing it. Then just like how it started, it stopped. I was back to an extreme sobbing. This pain wasn't just emotional anymore. I felt pins and needles in every limb of my body, and my ribs hurt. I just grabbed both of her cold hands and laid my head on her chest.

"Get a grip!" That's what I was telling myself. I took one large gasp for air. More like a yawn. And stopped crying. For the last time ever, I gave her a kiss on her forehead. If you were as close to me as EJ you probably would have heard "I love you more." It was a thing me and Elaine had. Who loves who more. I guess I won by default.

I turned around. It took everything in me to do so. I continued to walk outside. I didn't want to speak to anyone.

EJ was still kneeling next to Elaine's body. I told him to take his time and that I'd be in the car.

When I got in the car I opened the box Marcie gave me. She told me to wait till I got home but I needed something to take my mind away from the past hour. Inside the box was a necklace. It was silver and had a small charm of an angel. There was also a note in it. The note contained two simple messages. The first was that this necklace stayed with Marcie through many hard times. The second simply said "You know where to find me." My heart skipped a beat. I put the necklace on and clenched it. EJ got in the car and I immediately turned to hug him. He was crying. Not as bad as I was but worse than I've ever seen before.

The drive home went by quickly. I still felt sad and broken, but seeing Elaine's body, so peaceful, I was able to say goodbye to her. It felt like a weight was lifted off me.

We were back at EJ's and I went straight up to my room. I know EJ did the same. He looked so tired. I just took my pants off and slept in my t-shirt. I had no will power at all to change, or to shower. Going to sleep was getting easier each night it was just the mornings I was afraid of.

Chapter Seven: Jack

Melissa was back to her usual self. After Michael killed Matthew's sister she stopped being so bossy. She was back now. And she was making me do things again. Forcing me to do her dirty work. And it's like no matter what I do all of the ramifications fall on me. I go behind Matt's back, I can't be in control. I don't listen to Melissa's EVERY WHIM I don't get to be in control. With her it's conformity or nothing.

She was making me run away. As if it couldn't get worse she wanted me to do it in the middle of the night. And now she figured out how to talk to me while I'm in control. It's just another way for her to make sure everything goes her way.

It gave me chills thinking about getting on a train, at night, alone. If you haven't noticed I have really bad anxiety. And Melissa doesn't seem to understand—or care.

"There's a packed backpack underneath the bed." I heard her say it so clearly. It was like she was hovering over me. I don't know how she can do these things. How she can sense what we feel or stop us from being in control. Neither Michael or me can do it. It's completely unfair.

"Where's the knife?" I asked. There's no way I'm going out of the safety of this house, in the middle of the night without any weapon.

"In the front pocket of the bag. Now hurry up." She told me to go to the bank down the street and use the ATM machine to withdraw money. She wouldn't tell me what her plan was, but I just wanted to be out of it already.

I snuck out of the house pretty easily. It was creepy though, with all of the creaks in the floors and the complete darkness.

Evidently unlike Melissa I had compassion and I felt bad about leaving EJ.

When I was walking down the street I thought I had eternal goosebumps. It seems like they never go away. I decided to walk under the street lights so that I could see my surroundings at all times. I was walking so slow because every few seconds I heard something in the distance.

I could see the silhouette of the ATM machine in the distance, it was illuminating the dark. It was the only ATM that allowed large amounts of withdrawals. Melissa obviously did her homework.

When I got over to it, Melissa started shouting random numbers. Eventually I figured out what the numbers were for.

"Take out ten thousand and put it in the backpack." It took me forever to load all of the money into the bag. It made me feel so sly and dirty too. Melissa and Michael were only causing trouble and I couldn't stand it anymore. All I wanted was to be out of this situation. To be able to make my own decisions.

Melissa shouted to me, "Now go to the train station and get on the next train to Lakewood."

What was the train going to be like? I was scared to death the last time I was on a bus. And that was in broad daylight.

It was late at night, but I saw a taxi coming down the street. There were a few bars down on the main line so that's where they're probably coming from. My hands were shaking when I hailed the taxi. The driver could be an axe murderer for all I know. My mind always plays the worst scenarios. I hopped in and put my hood up.

"T-train station p-please." I don't know why I always stutter when I talk to other people. The only person I didn't stutter around was Matthew's sister, Elaine. She always made me feel safe. She could always tell the difference between all of us too. I was really upset when Melissa told me Michael killed her. I think Melissa was upset a little too. That's why she won't let Michael be in control anymore. The only reason she's letting me, is because I do what she says. It's not fair, and Matthew can't stop her anymore. He's not strong enough. He wasn't that strong before, that's why me, Melissa and Michael were created. He used to at least be able to control Melissa and Michael though.

I was at the train station now, and it seemed eerie. There was almost no one here and the station was very low lit. I handed the driver thirty dollars and got out of the car quickly. People scared me, so I didn't like being around them.

There was so much stuff in my backpack I started to feel the weight of the straps on my shoulders. I tried not to mind it and just went to buy a ticket.

There was only one booth open and the employee working it was sleeping. I tapped lightly on the glass window and the employee woke up quickly. He looked startled and asked me what I needed.

"C-can I h-have a ticket f-for Lakewood? P-please?" He looked at me like I had two heads.

"The next train leaves in ten minutes. That'll be fifty-six ninety-five." I reached in my bag and grabbed a one-hundred-dollar bill. I'm sure this made me look even sketchier. I could see my hand shaking as I gave it to him.

"Keep t-the change." He sighed and took it from me. I guess he sees things like this every day. I walked down a long hall to get to Terminal A. It smelled like sewage because it was underground. The lights were flickering on and off like a scene in a horror movie. My heart was beating so fast.

I saw the train in the distance and they were calling for the last passengers. I ran to get on the train and I was the only person on there. I went all the way to the back, curled into a seat, and fell asleep

———

Light was shining through my eyelids and there was a gentle tapping on my shoulder.

"Hello. Hello?" I turned and saw a man hovering over me. I jumped out of my seat. I don't particularly like it when strangers touch me.

"We're at Lakewood you have to get off the train now sir." The air here was crystal clear and it was humid outside.

Chapter Eight: Melissa

Up until now I didn't give much thought about what was going to happen from here. I just knew we needed to be out of Devon. It was for the best. Matthew would have never done it.

When I turned around there was a sign that said "'Motel Carla' north." That was my next destination. I hopped on the shuttle bus going that way. It was disgusting—all types of public transportation are disgusting—but this was horrible. It was beaten down and it smelled like a raging dumpster fire. And to top it all off I was extremely famished.

The bus was deserted which was a plus because I wasn't looking forward to having human interactions at the moment. The bus driver looked at me and said something, but I wasn't paying attention.

I threw a twenty-dollar bill at the bus driver and walked to the back. "You can keep the change." I said. I sat down and stared out the window. This led me to do the thing I hate most which is think. Not because it's a hard thing to do. Trust me, I'm much smarter than the others, but because then I start to feel *regret*. It was the worst feeling in the world. I couldn't help but actually feel bad for Matthew. And what was worse, I felt bad for EJ. I had always had a fixed opinion about him. He was a dead beat to me. Then seeing him—so broken—it changed my opinion. Not a lot but still. I felt kind of bad. And now I took Matthew away from him. It's for the best. It's for the best. It's for the best. That's what I'm going to keep telling myself anyway.

The jaunt to the motel was short and painful but I stuck it out. I noticed so many health code violations, but I decided not to say anything.

The outside of the motel looked "shabby". There was really no other word to describe it. The sign outside glowed faintly, and the roof looked like it was close to caving in. The sunlight reflected on the grey tinted windows. There was a door on the bottom floor that said "Directory" so I went there. It was smoky and dusty. I wasn't holding up too much hope for the rooms at this point.

I rang the bell on the desk and dust blew out from under it. An old man came threw a curtain in the back. He was walking slow, and I was already impatient as it is.

"Hello." I said impatiently. "I need a room for ten days."

"'Two hundred dollars.'" He said in a very harsh voice. He sounded like he was smoking since Christ was a child. He had an accent too. I think it's Russian but I'm not sure. He was older and had a white shirt with black stains all over it. I went in to the backpack, which by the way was extremely heavy, and pulled out two two-hundred-dollar bills.

"Your room is number 220."

"Two twenty?" Just to make sure I asked again. This doesn't look like the type of place you would want to get lost in.

"Yes." He replied as if I annoyed him. You can bet that when I leave this wretched place there will be a call placed to a health inspector. I just sighed loudly, took my key, and went upstairs to my room. There was a bed, a desk, a mini fridge and a television. I opened the blinds to let light into the room. The floor had yellow and red stains. I scowled at the sight of this room and turned to lock the door. I made sure that no one would be able to enter.

Oh lord, I hope the bathroom is semi clean. I need a shower very badly. My hands are black just from being in this filthy motel.

Finally, I got a reprieve. The bathroom looked pretty decent. Aside from the hideous pink tiling, it seemed clean.

I ripped off the clothes on my body along with the dirt they had acquired and threw them on the floor.

Seeing myself without clothes only reminded me how much I hate being in this body. Every time I look down it's just a constant reminder I'm in a man's body. The others think they have it tough, but they have no idea what it's like. On top of always having the constant feeling of having to protect Matthew, I'm a woman in a man's body. I have men's genitals and a man's voice. Elaine was the only one who understood. Yes, she loved Matthew, but she cared about the rest of us too. She was kind to me and would let me wear her clothes and her makeup whenever I was in control. She even bought a pair of heels in Matthew's size for me—I still have no idea how she found them since Matthew is like a size 14 in shoes.

And now that Michael decided to murder her I'm stuck having to take care of Matthew alone. It would help if he even liked me, but he hates me. He thinks I'm doing everything to hurt him. I'm just doing what's *right*.

The water felt good on my back. It was relaxing. My body went numb under it's pressure. I loved feeling clean. I also noticed the necklace Marcie gave to Matthew. I usually don't wear silver, this was beautiful though.

When I got out of my shower I realized I had little clothes packed. It was so unlike me to do that. I'm always prepared.

There was a strip mall down the street that I could go to to get some things.

I threw on the last pair of clean clothes I had packed and ran out the door. Since I'm clearly competent I made sure to lock the door and hide the bag before I left. I just took a couple of hundred dollars with me.

The walk to the mall only took about ten minutes but my feet were throbbing in pain. The road I walked on was so hot and rocky. I could feel my feet blistering.

I could get used to this town. It was quiet and even better there aren't many people around. I was in total bliss.

Even if I wasn't satisfied, there would be no other choice. Sooner or later the police will figure out that Matthew's hands were used to kill Elaine and they will send him away. There's no way we would survive prison—there's no way I could survive in prison.

The store was small. There was one lady at the cash register. I'm pretty sure she was asleep.

I took in every moment of being here. I never got to shop on my own. It was amazing and liberating. Not the store, it was kind of a dump, but you take what you can get in a town like this.

At first, I was going to go on a shopping spree for just myself, but I decided to do a good deed for once. I bought Matthew three pairs of jeans, a pair of sweatpants, and four shirts. I made sure to get them in all solid colors so that he could match without trying.

The others are horrible at color coordination. Then I picked a few things out for myself.

I checked myself out and left the money on the counter since the lady decided to not wake up.

I went back to the motel and changed into one of the dresses I bought. It felt so good to be in feminine clothes for once.

My evening got even better though when I found out that the TV had Judge Judy. I just sat and watched that for hours. Occasionally clapping and screaming at the people. Before I went to sleep I changed into other clothes in case I wasn't in control tomorrow morning. I drifted to sleep thinking about the peaceful day I had. Hopefully I'll have more like this....

Chapter Nine: Michael

Blood. There's blood everywhere. Every time I close my eyes I see Elaine's blood.　　　　I didn't want to kill her. I never wanted to hurt her. I just wanted her to love me. I wanted us to be more than just *friends*, but EJ was always getting in the way.

The whole reason I had that pocket knife was to scare EJ. I thought I could get him to stop seeing her. Or get him out of the picture somehow. But then Elaine found out and she was threatening to tell Matthew. And she got really mad and she was saying so many different things. She said we could never be together. Then she tried to make me take some medicine, so Matthew would be in control. Then called me stupid. I hate it when people call me that. I got so angry and I just... I just... I stabbed her. I ran out and tried to call 911 on someone else's phone but the guy got mad and beat me up. then I blacked out. I wish I could go back. I wish I could have saved her. I wish I could have stopped myself.

And Melissa. WHO THE HELL DOES SHE THINK SHE IS? Who let her be the boss of who gets to be in control. She is part of the reason I was so angry. She was taunting me. Just like she always does.

"Don't do anything stupid Michael." It was Melissa speaking to me. How was she talking to me? It doesn't matter. She's pissing me off though! I'm sick of her and Matt and everyone else always trying to control me. I'll do whatever I want!

"Don't go anywhere!" She just kept giving me orders.

"GET OUT!" I threw the T.V. remote at the wall and slapped my head into my palms. Breathe in, breathe out. That's what Dr. Walker used to tell me to do. It's a bunch of bull actually. It doesn't work, and it never did.

I need to get out of this crappy motel. I need to go out. I need alcohol. Melissa never lets me drink but I don't care. I'm going anyway.

"Don't do anything irrational." Melissa said. I know she was mocking me though. That's just who she is. She always made fun of me for not being the smartest.

I looked around me and saw a backpack in the corner. It was open and there was money hanging out of it. I went over and grabbed a one-hundred-dollar bill. I never held this much money before. No one ever really trusted me to.

There was a key on the table next to me, so I took that too and left. The motel was smoky. There was an old man sitting behind the counter.

"Excuse me man? Do you know if there's any bars around here, or anywhere I can get alcohol?" I tried to sound nice. He looked at me weird.

"Make a left then walk a few streets down until you see a place called Charlies."

"Ok, thanks dude." When I left I heard him say "That guy is so damn needy" under his breathe. The first thing I thought of was

Melissa. She's the neediest and pickiest person I know.

"Are you sure you can handle that many directions at once." Melissa was still in my head. Again, I slapped myself. This time a lot harder. She was starting to make me really angry. I could feel my face starting to get red. When I get mad I get jumpy and really red.

"I've given the matter some thought, and I'd think it would be in all of our best interests if you don't go." She said. She said it so smart too. Like she was the queen or something.

NO! She wasn't going to take this from me. I've been going through just as much as she has, but I don't get to relax? I don't get to have some time to myself? She goes on a shopping spree and I have to twiddle my thumbs in a hotel room.

She was making me so mad. And she's still taunting me and laughing at me.

"I don't say things I don't mean, and I'm pretty sure I told you to go back so GO!" She said. Again, with the rude tone. She thinks she's better them me. She thinks she's better then everyone.

Then for once I had a smart idea. I'm going to tell Matthew I killed Elaine. I'm going to tell him we ran away. I'm going to tell him everything. Then Melissa will be the one in trouble. Shell be the one who has to pay. Matthew will make sure she doesn't get to be in control. Ill be the one laughing then.

I kept slapping my head. I don't know for sure if it works but Melissa wasn't buzzing in at all.

I'm telling you she's going to get what's coming to her. That's what I keep saying to myself. It was actually making me calmer.

When I got back to the motel I wrote everything down on a piece of paper. I never wrote a letter, or anything for that matter before, so I just winged it.

"Hi Matthew, It's Michael. I'm just going to be straightforward with you. I killed Elaine. It's a long story and I didn't mean too. But anyway, Melissa made us come here. We're in Lakewood and you have to stop her. She's controlling everything. And she also took out all of your savings. The money is in the backpack. Please do something."

I set the note on the table and screamed Matthew's name. It helps him get in control. It worked once before for Elaine when I was on a rampage. Dr. Walker taught Elaine it. If only she used it the other night. I probably wouldn't be here right now.

I yelled his name over and over again.

"COME ON MATT! Get in control!" I took a breath. Then continued. I was shouting as loud as I could.

"MATTHEW   GREENE!   MATTHEW GREENE!"

Chapter Ten: Matthew

I was sweating. My feet were sore. I could hear my name crescendo in my head. I must've not been in control for a while because I have no idea where I am. It looks like a studio apartment, or a motel room.

I know something is wrong. There was only one other time I was forced into being in control, and it wasn't good.

There was a note on the nightstand directly in front of me. It looked like it was written in a rush. I picked it up and read it. I think my mouth dropped to the floor. MICHAEL KILLED ELAINE! There were other words but it's like those were the only ones I could see. I stopped reading there. I could feel my heart start skipping beats. Why would he? Tears were slowly coming down my face now. The thought that my own hands were used to hurt her. To mutilate her. It crippled me. No, it consumed me. My hands were shaking vigorously while I tried to read the rest of the note.

Ok, Melissa ran away and took all of Elaine's money. I said to myself calmly: Everything is *ok*. Except everything's not ok. My life is literally in shambles. Every time I feel like I can finally breathe something pulls me right back to square one. I just need to keep myself composed.

WAIT! What about EJ? I thought. I just left him. I killed my sister and left the only person I have in my life stranded. But I can't go back. I couldn't ever look him in the eyes. My hands are still shaking, and tears are still streaming down my face.

Seeing my hands rattle reminded me of how my Mom's used to. When she was really bad on drugs her whole body would shake. Then she would just take more drugs to try and stop it.

I crumbled the note and threw it on the floor. There was a backpack in the corner filled with money. I wouldn't care if it was my money. But it was Elaine's. Even though she's dead, I mean gone, it was still hers. She worked so hard for every damn dime, and the others don't even care. They totally disregarded everything. It infuriated me.

I decided on mailing the money to EJ. He deserves to have it. In total there was about ninety-five hundred. I kept five hundred just to help me get by. I have no idea what I'm going to do next. Well actually, that's a lie. I have an idea, I'm just not sure if I can go through with it.

There was a box with cleaning supplies under the sink in the bathroom. I took them out and packaged the money securely in the box. While I was in the bathroom. I saw myself in the mirror. I've seen myself before in mirrors, but this was different. Looking at myself only made me realize how much I really hate myself. Seeing myself like this sealed my fate. I couldn't handle looking at myself ever again. Not for the rest of my life. The image of myself was branding itself into my brain now.

I left my room to try and find someone who knows where I should go to mail the box. The entire building smelled like cigarettes and about half of the lights don't work.

At the desk was an older man. He was covered in black stains. I asked if he had a postage stamp and where there was a mailbox. He just stared at me for a while. I was too frantic to feel awkward, or to be polite.

"Do you?" It wasn't like me to be rude and impatient, but honestly, I don't care. He handed me a page of stamps and told me there was a mailbox out front. I licked the stamp and placed it on the box. It also wasn't like me to put it on crooked. I have a bit of OCD for things like that. But again, I really don't care anymore. It gave me a paper cut on the tip of my tongue. I winced but then I payed it no mind.

On the box I wrote "from Matthew" and slipped it in the mailbox slot. Then I went back up to the room to call EJ. I'm praying that he doesn't answer. I couldn't bear hearing his voice.

Thankfully he didn't. I left him a message. I know it's a terrible thing to do. To tell him about everything that's happened over the phone. I told him that it was Michael who killed Elaine. Then I told him that I had mailed him nine thousand dollars and that I was in Lakewood. The hardest thing I had to tell him though was that he's going to be too late when he comes. By the time the phone rang though I was sobbing again. Just knowing that it may hurt him even more, once again crippled me from the inside out. I wish I never existed. I wish Elaine was still alive. But I can't turn back time. And I certainly can't go on. I'm not strong enough nor do I even want to be. Not with what I know now. Most of all, I can't go on in a world where I killed my sister. A world where she's not here. I thought I could be strong, but I can't. And all of that stuff about how "It's what they would want," and "it gets easier day by day," it's… it's bullshit! It doesn't get better everyday. I wake up in the morning and for one second, I feel fine. I feel like my life isn't in pieces. Then it hits me. I just can't take it anymore.

Anymore, my life was literal despair. Just when I think I'm going to burst into a million pieces, it doesn't happen. I live another day. The only time I feel like I'm catching a breath is when I'm not in control. I can't not be in control though. I can't trust the others not to destroy my life further. *If it can be destroyed any further.*

The unequivocal truth: I can't live anymore. That's the sum of my life. Seventeen years of pain and suffering. Basically, my entire life was a cosmic joke if you really think about it. I go from one period of suffering to another. What made it worse, in between my "periods of suffering" was a sliver of happiness, that got stripped away from me. Without any warning signs. It was like the universe was laughing at me.

There was one last thing I needed. A cheeseburger. They were Elaine's favorite. I needed to do something for her. I owed her it. I don't know what it is, but I think a part of me feels like I'm going to be forgiven by Elaine by doing this. Like I owe her this one thing.

I ordered from room service. Not that it would be good. Their kitchen probably doubles as a bathroom. But I don't care. I want it to be the last thing I eat.

The burger came. I asked him to put it on a tab. He looked at me oddly and then walked away.

I ordered it just how Elaine would. Lettuce, tomatoes and bacon, no onion and medium rare. It was extra rare, but I still ate it.

When I was done I left an envelope with money on the pillow to cover the balance of my stay.

———

The ground is far from the top of the roof. There is a cool breeze and tears are starting to build up in my eyes. I'm not really sad. I'm at peace with my decision. Sadly, the bad outweighs the good.

I was trying to pray now. It was something I hadn't given much thought to. Ever really. I'm not really sure what to pray for. I guess that I see Elaine. Yes. That's what I'm praying for. Now that I really had time to think, it's the reason I'm doing this. So, I can see her. If that's what happens in the afterlife, or whatever. I guess I was also praying for an afterlife. I also prayed for EJ. He deserves it. He deserves a break.

———

I was standing on the edge of the roof now. I had to be at least three stories high. One step and it would all be over. No more pain. I could hear Melissa, she was trying to stop me. Jack wanted to help me, and Michael, still, just wanted to hurt me. Their voices were fading. It was over. I won. They can't stop me, and they can't control me anymore.

I closed my eyes and heard them no more. A soft breeze hit my cheek.

I closed my eyes and thought of Elaine. Her gentle smile. It was warm and welcoming. She really was like an angel. Just seeing her in my memory makes this whole thing so much easier. I clenched the necklace Marcie gave me. Then I took a step and for once it was just me, Matthew, no one else and I was no longer *afflicted*. I felt Elaine's embrace the whole way down...